THE THUNDER STORM

How the rain pours
   And the lightnings flash!
How the wind roars
   And the thunders crash!
But my little baby is safe as can be
Cuddling here on mother's knee.

ACKNOWLEDGEMENTS

The publisher wishes to thank all of the artists who graciously donated their artwork for this project.

Very special thanks to Coles Bookstores and Smithbooks for their generous support.

Thanks also to See Spot Run for donating the photography of the artwork on pages 8-9, 18-19, 26-27, 48-49, 56-57, 58-59 and 60-61; and to Ian Crysler for donating the photography of the artwork on pages 14-15.

The illustrations on pages 1, 2, 4, 6 and 64 were done by C.W. Jefferys for an early Canadian "Mother Goose", *Uncle Jim's Canadian Nursery Rhymes* by David Boyle, published by the Musson Book Company, Toronto and London, 1908. We are grateful to the Osborne Collection of Early Children's Books, Toronto Public Library, for the loan of this material. Reprinted with permission of the C.W. Jefferys Estate Archive.

The publisher gratefully acknowledges the assistance of the Canada Council, the Ontario Arts Council and the Ontario Ministry of Culture, Tourism and Recreation.

Groundwood Books/Douglas & McIntyre
585 Bloor Street West
Toronto, Ontario M6G 1K5

Canadian Cataloguing in Publication Data

Mother Goose
Mother Goose: a Canadian sampler

ISBN 0-88899-213-0

1. Nursery rhymes, English. 2. Children's poetry, English 1. Title.

PZ8.3.M67Mo 1994   j398.8   C94-931094-8

Design by Michael Solomon
Printed and bound in Hong Kong by
Everbest Printing Co., Ltd.

MOTHER GOOSE

A Canadian Sampler

*For the benefit of the
Parent-Child Mother Goose Program,
Toronto, Ontario*

FOREWORD BY
Celia Barker Lottridge

A GROUNDWOOD BOOK

DOUGLAS & McINTYRE

Toronto/Vancouver/Buffalo

Foreword

Nursery rhymes are treasures belonging to us all. They give us joy when we are young and later, when we think we have outgrown them, we discover images and phrases from the rhymes everywhere around us — in book titles and advertising slogans, layered into poetry, in political cartoons and in our everyday conversation. The clock strikes one, the cow jumps over the moon, and home we go again, jiggety-jig.

In this book you will rediscover these old friends and find new treasures, for the world of traditional rhyme seems to have no end. There are echoes of myth and observations of nature, eccentric characters and little human dramas, total nonsense and words to enjoy for their own sake. The origins of the rhymes are often lost, but they include popular songs and games, political satires, scraps of remembered history, wise sayings and street vendors' jingles. The fact that these rhymes live and flourish in our day is a tribute, not to their historical nature, but to their amazing ability to evoke vivid images and encourage playfulness.

The clocks and cows and moons you will meet in these pages have been newly pictured by a fine array of Canadian illustrators, each of whom has given fresh dimension to an old rhyme. From the satisfyingly realistic to the completely fantastical, these illustrations demonstrate beyond a doubt that Mother Goose rhymes encourage wonderful freedom of the imagination.

These pictures and the words that inspired them are meant to be shared between children and adults, for this is literature for the youngest age, when children rely on their parents, grandparents and other friendly adults to give them the words and pictures they love. And the best part is that it is so much fun for everyone.

Reading this book together with a child, for instance, is a perfect shared experience. The words and pictures of each rhyme make a story, so short that it can be lingered over and savoured. Children will quickly find favourites to be turned to again and again. And they will discover new favourites as they grow and change.

And there are other ways to share the rhymes. After all, these bits of poetry have been passed along orally for generations and have survived largely because they contain elements that delight and comfort little children. The rhythm of the words can accompany soothing rocking or lively bouncing. The words themselves often suggest actions that add a whole dimension of delight. Watching a child enjoy the fingers creeping up her arm while gleefully anticipating the tickle to come is a pleasure no adult should miss. In fact, noticing how children, no matter how young, are fascinated by the images in the pictures and calmed, distracted or stimulated by the rhythms and actions of the words will be an ongoing joy and resource to the adults involved.

Nursery rhymes are indeed treasures. We are lucky, we adults, for in sharing the rhymes with our children we can rediscover their richness for ourselves.

Celia Barker Lottridge

Con

n t s

Pussy cat, pussy cat, where have you been?
 I've been to London to look at the queen.
Pussy cat, pussy cat, what did you there?
 I frightened a little mouse under her chair.

Round and round  the garden

Like a teddy bear;

One step, two step,

Tickle you 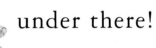 under there!

*Hold the baby's hand and trace circles
around her palm with your finger.
Slowly walk your fingers up her arm.
Then quickly tickle her under the arm.*

Knock  at the door,

Ring the bell,  Peek in,

 Lift up the latch,  Walk in,

Go downstairs and eat apples!

Knock gently on the baby's forehead.
Tug a lock of his hair and look into his eyes.
Brush the tip of his nose and touch his lips.
Run your fingers down to his tummy. Then tickle.

D. PERNA

When the wind is in the east
'Tis neither good for man nor beast,
When the wind is in the north
The skilful fisher goes not forth,
When the wind is in the south
It blows the bait in the fish's mouth;
When the wind is in the west
Then 'tis at the very best.

Father and Mother and Uncle John
Went to market one by one,
Father fell off,
Mother fell off
But Uncle John went on and on and on and on . . .

The Man in the Moon looked
 out of the moon,
Looked out of the moon
 and said,
"'Tis time for all children
 on the earth
To think about getting to bed!"

Three blind mice. See how they run! They all ran after the farmer's wife, who cut off their

tails with a carving knife. Did you ever see such a sight in your life? Three blind mice.

Slowly, slowly, very slowly
Goes the garden snail,
Slowly, slowly, very slowly
Up the garden rail.

Quickly, quickly, very quickly
Runs the little mouse,
Quickly, quickly, very quickly
To his little house.

To market, to market,

to buy a fat pig,

Home again, home again, dancing a jig.

To market, to market, to buy a fat hog,
Home again, home again, jiggety-jog.

Kith

23

The moon is round
As round can be,
Two eyes, a nose and a mouth
Like me!

Elsie Marley, grown so fine,
    Won't get up to feed the swine
But stays in bed till half past nine.
    Lazy Elsie Marley!

Sing a song of sixpence,
A pocket full of rye,
Four-and-twenty blackbirds
Baked in a pie!

When the pie was opened
The birds began to sing,
Was that not a dainty dish
To set before the king?

The king was in his counting-house
   Counting out his money,
The queen was in the parlour
   Eating bread and honey.

The maid was in the garden
   Hanging out the clothes,
When down came a blackbird
   And snapped off her nose.

Over in the meadow in the sand in the sun
Lived an old mother turtle and her little turtle one.
"Dig" said the mother. "We dig" said the one,
So they dug all day in the sand in the sun.

Over in the meadow where the stream runs blue
Lived an old mother fish and her little fishes two.
"Swim" said the mother. "We swim" said the two,
So they swam all day where the stream runs blue.

Over in the meadow in a hole in a tree
Lived an old mother owl and her little owls three.
"Tu-whoo" said the mother. "Tu-whoo" said the three,
So they tu-whooed all day in a hole in a tree.

Over in the meadow by the old barn door
Lived an old mother rat and her little ratties four.
"Gnaw" said the mother. "We gnaw" said the four,
So they gnawed all day by the old barn door.

Over in the meadow in a snug beehive
Lived an old mother bee and her little bees five.
"Buzz" said the mother. "We buzz" said the five,
So they buzzed all day in a snug beehive.

Jan Thornhill

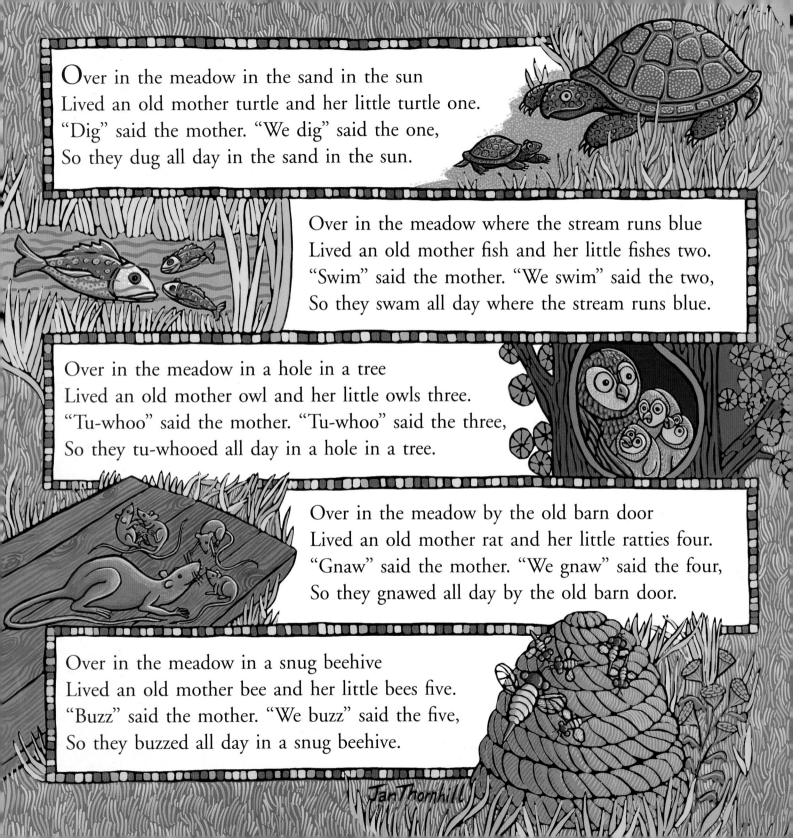

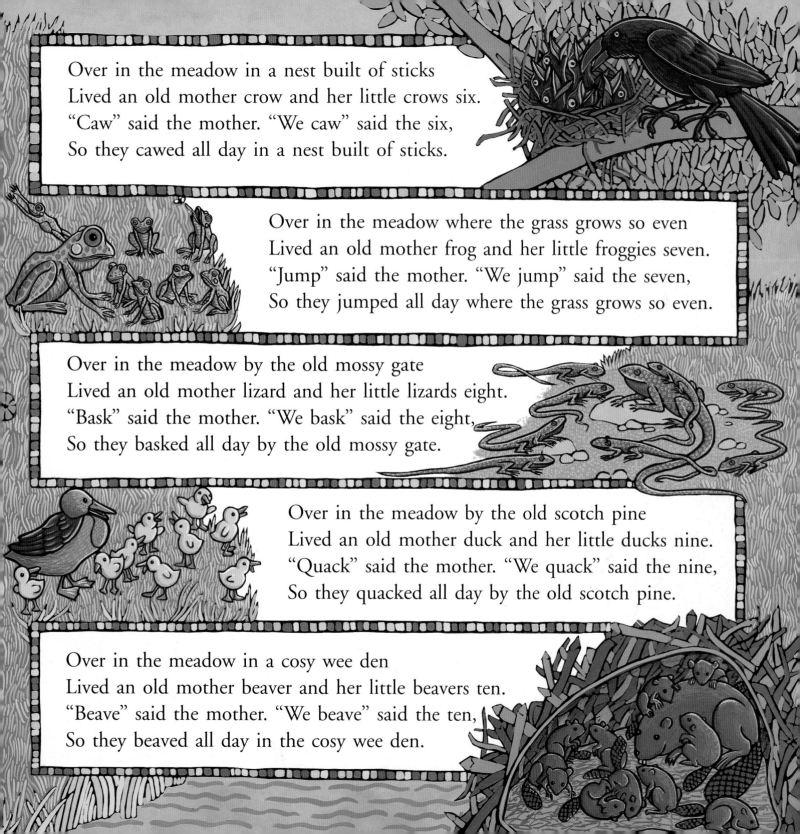

Over in the meadow in a nest built of sticks
Lived an old mother crow and her little crows six.
"Caw" said the mother. "We caw" said the six,
So they cawed all day in a nest built of sticks.

Over in the meadow where the grass grows so even
Lived an old mother frog and her little froggies seven.
"Jump" said the mother. "We jump" said the seven,
So they jumped all day where the grass grows so even.

Over in the meadow by the old mossy gate
Lived an old mother lizard and her little lizards eight.
"Bask" said the mother. "We bask" said the eight,
So they basked all day by the old mossy gate.

Over in the meadow by the old scotch pine
Lived an old mother duck and her little ducks nine.
"Quack" said the mother. "We quack" said the nine,
So they quacked all day by the old scotch pine.

Over in the meadow in a cosy wee den
Lived an old mother beaver and her little beavers ten.
"Beave" said the mother. "We beave" said the ten,
So they beaved all day in the cosy wee den.

Hoddley, poddley, puddle and fogs,
Cats are to marry the poodle dogs;
Cats in blue jackets and dogs in red hats,
What will become of the mice and rats?

Hey diddle diddle
   The cat and the fiddle,
The cow jumped over the moon;
   The little dog laughed
   To see such sport
And the dish ran away with the spoon.

A was an apple-pie
B bit it
C cut it
D dealt it
E eat it
F fought for it
G got it
H had it
J joined it
K kept it
L longed for it
M mourned for it

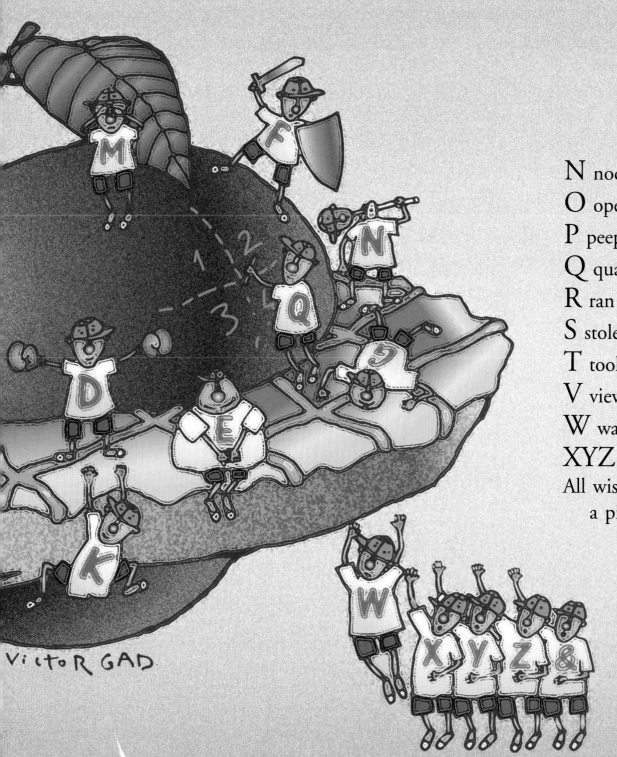

N nodded at it
O opened it
P peeped in it
Q quartered it
R ran for it
S stole it
T took it
V viewed it
W wanted it
XYZ & ampersand
All wished for
   a piece in hand.

Fishes swim in water clear,
Birds fly up into the air,
Serpents creep along the ground,
Boys and girls run round and round.

Kady MacDonald Denton

38

There was an old woman tossed up in a basket
　Seventeen times as high as the moon;
Where she was going I couldn't but ask it,
　For in her hand she carried a broom.

Old woman, old woman, old woman, quoth I,
　O whither, O whither, O whither, so high?
To brush the cobwebs off the sky!
　Shall I go with thee? Ay, by and by.

41

I had a little nut tree,
Nothing would it bear
But a silver nutmeg
And a golden pear;
The King of Spain's daughter,
She came to see me
And all because of my little nut tree.

I skipped over water,
I danced over sea
And all the birds in the air couldn't catch me.

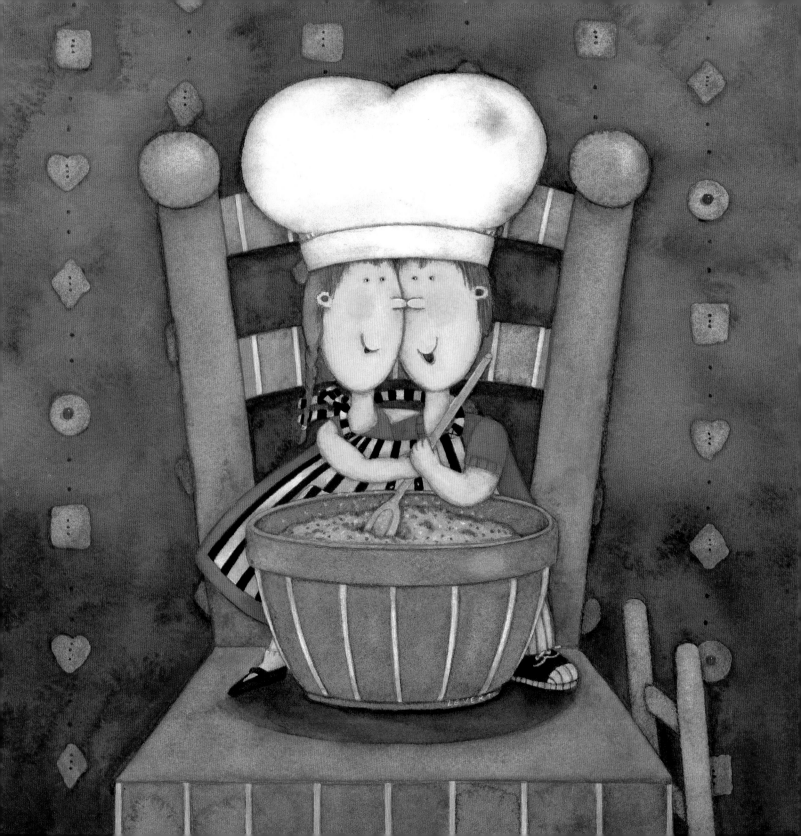

Mix and stir and pat in the pan,
I'm going to make a gingerbread man
With a nose so neat
And a smile so sweet
And gingerbread shoes on his gingerbread feet.

Robins

A robin and a robin's son
Both went to town to buy a bun,
They couldn't decide on plum or plain

And so they went back home again.

Jack be nimble,
Jack be quick,
Jack jump over
The candlestick.

My mother said
That I never should
Play with the gypsies
In the wood.
If I did
She would say,
Naughty girl to disobey.
Your hair shan't curl,
Your shoes shan't shine,
You naughty girl
You shan't be mine.
My father said
That if I did
He'd bang my head
With the teapot lid.

50

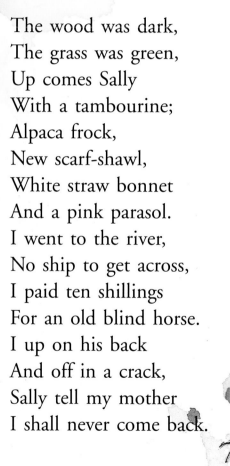

The wood was dark,
The grass was green,
Up comes Sally
With a tambourine;
Alpaca frock,
New scarf-shawl,
White straw bonnet
And a pink parasol.
I went to the river,
No ship to get across,
I paid ten shillings
For an old blind horse.
I up on his back
And off in a crack,
Sally tell my mother
I shall never come back.

Catharine
O'Neill

Little Boy Blue, come blow your horn,
The sheep's in the meadow, the cow's in the corn.
Where is the boy that looks after the sheep?
He's under the haystack fast asleep!
Will you wake him?
No, not I
For if I do
He's sure to cry.

53

There was an old woman who lived in a shoe,
   She had so many children she didn't know what to do,
She gave them some broth without any bread
   And whipped them all soundly and put them to bed.

Polly put the kettle on,
Polly put the kettle on,
Polly put the kettle on,
We'll all have tea.

Sukey take it off again,
Sukey take it off again,
Sukey take it off again,
They've all gone away.

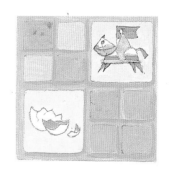

Humpty Dumpty sat
on a wall,

Humpty Dumpty had
a great fall,

All the king's horses
and all the king's men

Couldn't put Humpty
Dumpty together again.

FRANKLIN HAMMOND

60

Hickory, dickory, dock,
The mouse ran up the clock.
The clock struck one,
The mouse ran down,
Hickory, dickory, dock.

61

I saw a ship a sailin',
   A sailin' on the sea
And oh, it was laden
   With pretty things for thee.

There were comfits in the cabin
   And apples in the hold,
The sails were made of silk
   And the masts were made of gold.

Four and twenty sailors
   That sat upon the deck
Were four and twenty white mice
   With chains about their necks.

The captain was a duck
   With a packet on his back,
And when the ship began to move
   The captain cried, "Quack! quack!"

Index of Illustrators